D.R.I.N. is native of Conecuh County. A graduate of Evergreen High School, he also went to Reid State Technical College to further his studies and received an associate degree in Industrial Electricity and Electronics. The author is also a veteran but is best known for his role as an actor in the film *Heaven Falls.*

To all family, friends, and fans – national
and international.

D.R.I.N. Nation

The Kingdom

The Empire

The Republic

The Confederation

The Federation

The Commonwealth

The Superpowers

The Polity

The Domain

P.S. This includes everyone regardless of who they are or
where they are from.

D.R.I.N.

Less Than Holy, The Victims, The Cries

Austin Macauley Publishers™
London • Cambridge • New York • Sharjah

Ordering Information:
Quantity sales: special discounts are available on quantity purchases by corporations, associations, and others. For details, contact the publisher at the address below.

Publisher's Cataloging-in-Publication data
D.R.I.N.
Less Than Holy, The Victims, The Cries

ISBN 9781643787824 (Paperback)
ISBN 9781643787817 (Hardback)
ISBN 9781645365167 (ePub e-book)

Library of Congress Control Number: 2019907951

www.austinmacauley.com/us

First Published (2020)
Austin Macauley Publishers LLC
40 Wall Street, 28th Floor
New York, NY 10005
USA

mail-usa@austinmacauley.com
+1 (646) 5125767

I would like to acknowledge my parents, Bobby and Ardella Palmore; and my kids, Raphel and Rickell Palmore.

D.R.I.N. – When a person experiences any or all, whether mentally or physically, Dreams, Realities, Imaginations, or Nightmares.

"Brother," the Older Brother asked, "will you be my keeper? Then walk with me; let us journey throughout, keeping and watching over each other, eating and drinking and not having any worries. Let us be self-made. Making ourselves Kings within the earth, but where shall we start first? Look, let us begin with the people, bringing forth our laws, bringing our structure to these people; but first, let us distance ourselves, to make laws to govern. Let our first act of law be to let the people know that we are the beginning and the ending. If any law is to be changed, then it will only be by our hand, and if anyone opposes, there will be consequences to them and their loved ones. We will appoint different men of all districts of the earth, officials of their birth districts, allowing them to be the one carrying out our laws.

"Let's make sure that then men populate every part of the earth, that the women should carry the seeds of these men of their district."

The Young Brother, having love for his Older Brother, agreed to this. Not having the heart and mindset of his Older Brother, he was naive to his brother's plot; now, while conversing with his Older Brother, he wanted to make good on his agreement and promised that he wanted to have more insight on different matters and issues.

In response, the Older Brother said, "Brother, worry not yourself on these matters. But I will see that things take place."

"Brother, leave me be so that I can start the process of setting these worries of yours straight," he said, having complete faith in his Older Brother.

He said to his Brother, "So be it, let me excuse myself from your presence. But know this, Brother, the things that will come together for you and me have not been known to men, and will never come to ruins."

Now, before leaving, the Younger Brother kissed his Older Brother on both cheeks, having no input on what was about to take place in his Older Brother's ways of doing things.

He watched his Younger Brother move out of sight until his very eyes had no visual. The Older Brother began immediately on finding a resting ground. So now, coming upon a resting place, the Older Brother erected a tent or some kind of living quarters to accommodate himself.

After a long day of conversing with his Younger Brother, the Older Brother retired himself in his living quarters for a good night's rest. Falling into a deep sleep, he began to dream. While dreaming, he was approached by something in the form of a man with a robe on, concealing his face.

The Older Brother shouted out, "Who are you, and what do you want with me?"

In response, the man-shaped form said, "I am your close ally. Someone who has your best interest in mind."

While observing the man, he thought to himself, '*The next question I ask must strike right to the heart of this man.*'

Now gazing at the man, the Older Brother asked, "What is my best interest and how does my best interest serve you?"

Once again, the man responded by answering his question with a question. "What is your name?"

So the Older Brother said, "I am known by my brother as 'Brother.'"

The man-shaped form said to him, "So is it not appropriate for me to call you 'Brother?'"

At this time, he was awakened by loud thunder and strong winds. Awaking from his dream, the Older Brother went on the outside of his tent, looking up at the sky and seeing the wind sweep across the land. He quickly checked his living quarters to make sure the tent was secure. After completing the things that were necessary to secure his resting area, he made his way back to the inside.

After making it inside, a violent storm approached. Heavy rain began to pour down, while the thunder and lightning had its way in the sky, the winds pushing against his tent.

The Older Brother sat silently, waiting on the violent storm to pass. While waiting, the Older Brother fell into a deep sleep once again.

He began to dream. The man-shaped form with his face concealed reappeared. The Older Brother began to say, "I have considered what you said; I do wish and find it appropriate for you to call me 'Brother,' since you, out of your own mouth, say that you are my ally and have my best interest in mind."

So then the man-shaped form with the concealed face said, "Brother, I will construct ways so you can govern the people and rise as King to the people."

This made the Older Brother very joyful; he leapt for joy, but he recalled the only thing that he had love for was his Younger Brother.

Not feeling threatened nor harmed, in fact having built a relationship with the man-shaped form, he said to him, "Even though I am happy for this, I will need my Younger Brother by my side as a co-ruler."

He asked the Older Brother, "Tell me about your brother."

So he started telling him that the only person he had ever trusted and loved was his brother. "Even though he is my blood brother, he is different from me. My brother is naive, low with understanding, easily deceived and misled. He is often accounted for as being a good man, not being misunderstood as being something different."

After hearing all these things about the Younger Brother, he said to him, "Now, Brother, tell me, reveal all things about yourself. This is important in moving forward with things I will instruct you to do. Leave nothing out, so I can tell you how to punish all that oppose you being King."

So the Older Brother began to speak boldly about himself, saying, "I and my wants are one, having the flesh to act against other flesh, not sparing man, woman, nor child, showing no mercy, as my heart pains me. I inflict pain on others, putting my wants first, showing others to their tombstone by death, making my Young Brother a watcher of all my deeds, telling him he should have no mercy, that the best place for them is not to exist. But I, the Older

Brother, have failed in making him this man, even after the weak ones have deceased by my hands. I take hold of their possessions and, if possible, their dwelling places to be sold off for gold. These things that I do is a tribute to my wants, making my flesh have power over me in action, but the source of the flesh is my heart wanting more, taking pride in all my works. So I ask, do these things disgust you?"

The man-shaped form said to him, "Continue."

"When my Young Brother and I were infants, a heavy burden was placed on us. We saw with our very eyes, not the things that were bad; there was nothing parenting us on what was good. So I took charge on me and my Younger Brother by using things that were crafted for our very lives."

So the man-shaped form asked, "Which things of craft did you use?"

His voice went from speaking boldly to a humble tone when describing the different crafts he had to use.

"My first loves were those considered as liars, one who was deceiving and misleading in telling a story its falsification, leading the one being foolish, thrown for me to receive different things that were of a profit as I convinced them in my stories, leaving the feminine ones weeping while they were consoled by the one that was supposed to be the head. I practiced this day in and day out. I had subjection over many, without them seeing what was to be for me and not them. Their consequences were a way of reduction, while their minds became one to be beneficially controlled. They believed not even their own judgment of character, because I had persuaded them not to believe how they were to gain, if they only believe in what I said. It wasn't injustice from the mouth, it was being handed out to all that listened. Not brothers, sisters, mothers, or fathers could find fault in what was smooth talk. I truly say it was a double-edged sword, cutting its way through their hearts, leaving sound minds in confusion. This method was hard to detect. I kept manifesting myself as the one to be trusted. Look what was being manifested to me. Division of the people made it easy to steal what was left to be stolen; their hope.

"As I listen to them questioning hope, I took up the charge, becoming the head on this charge, furthering demonizing it, asking them, *'who has hope and what would they hope for?'* For many have hope, but with no return from hope, leaving them with only false beliefs. It returns with no work, no proof, because the people have not witnessed its work. We the people should not believe further, but abandon this way of thinking and not return to its practice, to hold on to such things will only further damage generations to come, so let us, the people, take a Declaration of Independence from hope. Now, while the other people took a stand of independence, another befriended me, taking their position as the friend of the Liar, wanting to know more about the friend of the Liar. In return, he said that everything he sold with lies, resting the weak ones in comfort. I collect. 'I am known as the Thief, stealing from all that rest their belief and possession with him. We work together, and in our accomplishment we cannot fail. One needing the other, working as one accord. Now be we, the Liar is your first lie. I befriended you to manifest myself to you. Even though we are different, we are the same.'

"In working together, completing the task at hand, because they entrusted the Liar with much. The appointed time came for me to steal, taking their hope and what faith was left, causing division, separation. Independence was their way of life, family against family, neighbor against neighbor, how they build generations of nations to withstand any obstacles. Destruction had befallen them all, now the things that had been stolen were given to me as a gift, not aware of their own action. But look, the Thief had been silenced by the one coming forward, an image, one unlike man, feminine, physical beauty, a woman inviting herself among me and the thief then introducing herself, introducing herself as the Adulteress. *'I am known as the Adulteress, the one who vowed to one but takes pleasure in many.'*

The Older Brother said, "What affair does one have with me and the Thief?"

In reply, she said, "It's not the Adulteress, Thief, and Older Brother who must come together; only the Older Brother and the Adulteress. The Thief can be relieved from among us."

Now, with smooth talk, she was seducing the Older Brother, striking at his heart with every venomous word in order to mislead him.

"I am the symbol and representative of love, building nations in this matter, birthing their children, leading men and likewise their sons from war." With every calculated step bringing the Older Brother closer to self-destruction by means of her own personal gain, touching him, saying, "Older Brother, is it not fitted for every man to experience love, and I come in the name of love."

Now, at this time, intercourse began to settle in his mind. Temptation began to spread throughout his body, paralyzing any other thoughts to intervene, as she began to circle the Older Brother. The seeds of deception began to blossom, furthering the advisement with a kiss until she bared all of her nakedness. What was mental became physical, both lust and pleasure was being fulfilled because they shared in physical pleasure

"I, the Older Brother, cannot deny the Adulteress opened my eyes to what love is and, because I had grown fond of her, she has become my mistress. The thing that was a one night stand became repetitious, I tell you this day, mistress, whatever adventures that I may encounter, you will be with me because you have grown deeply rooted in my heart, not physically but that in which you have planted in me: love."

Wanting to know more with the desire that burned inside of him, the Adulteress continuously kept his interest, saying, "Older Brother, because this will define who you are, I have separated myself from the very vow I took in order for you will be filled with this gift."

The next thing to be said was one that of disbelief, "Older Brother, when you have become receptive of all things, I, your mistress, will be no more. I will be that which I am, the Adulteress. I am what I am."

Now the Older Brother became angry, but, look, yet another presence was approaching, one that was very dark. What was anger turned to fear, because of fear he rejected this presence in his heart and mind, wanting freedom from this one. Evil and death accompanied the presence, not as his associate, but his slaves, him being their master. Because she, the Adulteress, was present and had not witnessed such vileness, she fell asleep in death instantly.

Standing there with a firm look and aggressive in speech, he said, 'Older Brother, I am known as the Murderer. Not having emotions, but separating all things in blood. I am unsearchable. In finding good in me, what thing can be shielded from me? I, the Murderer, take pleasure in wars. I was conceived from the hate of man, but was birthed through the first bloodshed of man, because I was made this way, immortality I reside in, not having no end. Older Brother, open your eyes to me and see the things I can do and have accomplished, because you have rejected me in your heart and mind, these things will not be granted to you. I am eternal, so accept me internally, so you will not be blind to the things you should see or be deaf to the things you should hear. Calm yourself in fear of me; unlike the Adulteress, I have concealed my vile acts and took a different look so you too won't fall asleep in death. Older Brother, do not be like the dead in their tombstones, unresponsive and unable to act."

At hearing this, the Older Brother was not blind, but seeing; and was not deaf, but hearing.

'The very things you are struggling with will cease, whether good or bad, respect and order will be. When you are in the midst of men, if any oppose, death will be their reward. Then who among them can speak, even those who came before me? Know me, the Liar, the Thief, and the Adulteress. Now, Older Brother, take what they taught you and let them become a part of you, also take me as the head, the dominant one of them all, and journey well.'

Upon hearing this, the Older Brother began to feel strange, different. What was forming up within him was foreign, something new, a new power.

He began to feel powerful to what had been said, falling to his knees, taking an oath, saying, "I, the Older Brother, by the powers invested in me, have charged all that inhabits the earth guilty by blood or association with self-interest, not being able to show interest beyond yourselves, self-claiming to be that which is good among others who among you have took in the Different Ones showing their acts of badness, well who among you showed willingness to steer them from badness. Strangers they were, and strangers you will be, only knowing your ways have I judge, because I have been chosen. What body of water, hill, valley, mountain, masses of people, or mass of land foreign or domestic will hide you? I do affirm that through me, their pain will be the Different Ones' pleasure, unleashing fleshly cries, I do affirm there will be no saving them, after all that will be done, I do affirm that the Different Ones will have their justice."

The Different Ones known as the Thief, Liar, Adulteress, and Murderer will have their victory.

Now rising up out of his sleep, the Older Brother found that his abode was in need for some much-needed repairs. He abandoned his abode in search for materials to repair his dwelling place. He secured the place with traps to keep out intruders, and to keep what he left behind safe. As he entered the wilderness to find supplies, he felt a sense of unwelcomeness. Conditions in the wilderness were impossible to any ordinary person, but because he took comfort in what the Murderer had told him, making the Different Ones a part of him there. There was nothing of fear about him, only to find the things that were needed for his dwelling place.

While making his way through thorn bushes in the wilderness, he was cautious and observant of what he felt and what he saw. The things he felt, came about from never having to go into an uninhabited place looking for such things, with no sense of security, only depending solely upon himself, the things he saw were more thorn bushes, trees, and trailless ways in and out of the wilderness.

Something caught his attention nearby. He closed in on this. Siting up on this tree were bones, skeleton, remains of what appeared to be a man.

He looked around to make sense of what caused the death of this man, only to find nothing of evidence, so he concluded that the man died from a lack of direction, driving the man to madness, taking his own life.

There was evidence of food and water near, but no proof of marking to keep him from getting lost in the wilderness. Seeing this, the Older Brother buried the remains and made a marking at his burial site, writing '*unknown.*' Not far from the man's skeleton was a different living quarters. Assuming this was a place that the dead man occupied, he searched through it, finding tools to take with him. Separating one tool from the others, this one with a sharp edge, he used it for the marking of the trees, so he and the unknown man wouldn't share the same fate.

Marking of the trees gave him a sense of direction. Not wanting to be captured and imprisoned by the wilderness, knowing that isolation was an enemy, worse than any physical opponents, being in a place left in its natural state, uncultivated, was no friend to anyone. While moving through the wilderness, making his marking, the Older Brother came in contact on the outside of the outer edge of this wilderness, with some sort of a man-made trail leading to a different place. Making his way through this trail with less resistance without the thick bush that heavily guarded this wilderness, a familiar sound was near. A sound of running water. As he drew closer, the sound became a sight. He approached the stream for a much-needed drink. While taking a drink from the stream of water that was at the outer edge of this wilderness, something else caught his attention; a valley, a valley that was between hills and mountains with more man-made trails. One that possibly led to civilization.

The Older Brother became joyed, but before he could further himself in another journey, the Older Brother took a much-needed rest beside the stream of running water.

He also began to reason with what happened in the wilderness, giving him further proof that civilization was on the other side, between or beyond the hills and mountains, saying to himself, 'The remains that I buried in the wilderness was more proof of other humans, the unknown man entry musts everyone from and through these valley to the stream of water; this would explain the water that was near, and the food must have come through a kill in the wilderness.'

After a time of reasoning with himself, the Older Brother decided to rest until the next day. Now after a night of resting, even though he desired to move forward toward the hills and mountain for further investigation of other human life, it was important, even feeling it was vital, for him to return to his abode because of the things of importance.

Now, as he began to make his way through the wilderness, following his trial of markings on the trees, he grew into hunger, an appetite for food. Yet what emerged was that which was already a part of him, the Murderer. The hungrier he became, the more forthcoming the Murderer was, until he was fully transformed into the Murderer and nothing else. It had sensed that the Older Brother was about to encounter great danger.

As he came to the edge of the wildernesses with his abode in view, what he saw was disturbing. He closed onto his living quarters, only to find that it had been sabotaged. Nothing of importance was in sight, but by chance there was something in sight; the intruder, the enemy. Not of man or of men, but one that moved with caution, vile looking, a wild beast that slithers about on his stomach as the wild beast moved closer. A giant serpent in search of food.

As the serpent took a stance to strike, the Older Brother, who had taken form of the Murderer because of what he sensed in the wilderness, yelled loudly to the wild beast: "I hunger." Then, with an aggressive voice, saying, "Beast, how many souls of men have you tasted? But on this day, it will be I that tastes your soul over a flaming fire."

Now, having the sharp edge tool beside him that was discovered in the wilderness, he asserted himself towards the beast with a violent blow to the head.

The serpent screamed violently, plunging to the ground, striking the Older Brother.

"Now, man-eater, your days have been accounted for."

As the giant serpent lay openly in death on the ground, the Older Brother began to behead the beast and remove the skin from the serpent, keeping the skin for a souvenir, but having no use for the head. He had lost things of importance to the beast; having his skin as a token was proper and rewarding for the Older Brother. As promised before the beast was killed by the brother, the man-eater was prepared, roasted over an open fire, then feasted on by the Older Brother. The thing that seemed minimum, of no importance, became something of importance.

During his feast, celebrating his kill of the beast, the Older Brother became ill. Sickness struck him to the ground, because when he struck the man-eater, poison began to spread throughout his body. At seeing this, the Older Brother, even though he felt feverish, started gathering up food from his feast and collected his skin of the serpent that he proudly owned, and began his journey back through the wilderness. He followed the markings he had made on the trees in order to keep him from getting lost.

Now making his way through the wilderness, he noticed something he hadn't notice before; a tree with berries on it. As he got off the trail of marked trees to gather up some of the berries, his fever became more intense. Moving back onto the trail, the Older Brother had deepened himself further into the wilderness to a familiar place; the stream of running water.

As he rested beside the stream, not being able to go any further, he began to hear a noise of footsteps moving toward him.

In a light voice, he said, "Who goes there?" as the Older Brother sat there, defenseless, not able to defend himself, he started to think of another foe, an enemy, with his sharp-edged tool beside him.

The footsteps became closer, but still nothing in his sight. Once again, with a light voice, the Older Brother said, "Who goes there?"

Because the poison had consumed the body of the Brother, he fell to the ground, passing out, only to be put to death by the poison of the enemy. Not yet passing over into death but in and out of consciousness, the steps stopped and were upon him. He was not able to make out the enemy because the poison had blurred his vision and left him without the ability to speak.

The Older Brother said, "Enemy, will you taunt me into death?"

Now the enemy took some of the berries that the Older Brother had gathered in the wilderness, and fed them to him slowly with sips of water from the stream. The Older Brother passed out. Repeating this day by day, the Older Brother showed signs of life with movements of the body, but he was still weak and speechless from the poison. More berries and water were added to his feeding to keep his flesh nourished. Now after four days of feeding and watering, the Older Brother made more movement. With some help, the Older Brother turned on his side. With his vision still being blur, he was able to determine the form of the enemy.

The enemy was a man. As the Older Brother tried to speak, the enemy that turned out to be a man silenced the Older Brother by putting his finger to his mouth, but continued nourishing the Older Brother with water and berries, telling him to rest.

While resting, slowly gaining his strength back, the Older Brother began to ask himself, *Who and why would any man aid me from death, the Older Brother?* This dazed and confused him in his resting position. As another day and night passed, more of his strength was gained, along with some of his sight and his ability to speak.

The Older Brother asked the stranger to help him stand, so the man helped him stand, then the Older Brother asked the stranger to come closer to him, so he did. As the man came into his vision, the Older Brother said to the man, "What a familiar face. Now look me in my eyes."

As the man looked the Older Brother in his eyes, both men began to say to the other one, "Is this possible? Could this be?"

Both became recognizable to each other. They laughed and wept, because this was a joyful moment. Who was thought to be the enemy, a man that was a stranger, was no one other than the Younger Brother.

As they laughed and wept some more, the Younger Brother said, "Brother, forgive me for being ignorant, not knowing my own brother."

The Older Brother said, "Stop, for much time has been passed between us, in fact I could be saying the same to you. I should have recognized my own Younger Brother under my circumstance, good or bad, so let me, the Older Brother, ask you for your forgiveness. Now, Younger Brother, let us put away this foolish talk, because much time has passed us already. The last time we saw each other, both of our appearances were different. So let us spend no time on asking for forgiveness, but instead let's make our time of importance; catching up on things that we encountered, endured, and overcame. So let us feast, celebrating near a fire on this day, eating from the food I had gathered but only for a little while, because the poison is still my blood. I need some much-needed rest to recover from this day of pain and pleasure, so eat, Younger Brother, and let your mouth make a joyful noise on things to come."

So before the Older Brother retired himself for his resting place, he ate and he began to rejoice on different things to come. "Younger Brother, before I position myself in a position to sleep, I, the Older Brother, ask what method you used to nourish me back from the grave."

The Younger Brother laughed and said, "Older Brother, I learned many things throughout my travel. It wasn't a method I used, but the things you ask about is in the berries. The power of life was in the berries. It is a cure, antidote for very poisonous animals of small and large size. This was showed and taught to me throughout different regions and districts so it wasn't something I did, but what the berries did."

Now at hearing this, the Older Brother and the Younger Brother began to laugh while securing the leftover food from the feast and maintaining and securing the fire they had made during their celebration.

The maintained and secured fire throughout the night kept them warm and warned off any unexpected visitors that would might harm them in their sleep.

The Younger Brother asked his final question for tonight; "Older Brother, about the berries. I thought you knew of their healing power."

In reply, their Older Brother said this; "The berries, I didn't…" before closing his eyes.

The night passed and day came. The younger and Older Brother woke from their sleeping position and greeted each other with a hug.

As another day and night passed, the Older Brother began to speak, saying, "Younger Brother, let's use this time to further ourselves in conversing about different things we have encountered while we were separated."

The Younger Brother began to speak, saying, "Older Brother, after we had departed from each other, I, the Younger Brother, became alone. Not being at the hand of my Older Brother…this by itself brought great strain on me, not being in the protection of my brother or being able to depend on him for food, clothing, and shelter. I, the Younger Brother, carried this burden with me from district to district, from region to region. This weight I carried always made me a victim of different circumstances, because I was low with understanding, wanting to be in my brother's presence. I always was an outsider in these places, foreign to their culture and their family because the only family I knew wasn't with me. That's you, Older Brother. With these difficulties came great pain, not only being responsible for me and my survival but for other families too, in each district and region of all of my travels."

As the Older Brother listened, he held his tongue and tightened his fingers into a fist, raging what was inside of him but still staying silent.

The Younger Brother continued in his talk. "Older Brother, I was enslaved by being low in understanding, so I became a slave to different families, taking whatever work or skill that I saw others do or would show me, whatever craft I was skilled at. The families received the larger payment and I received enough to survive for that day, to ensure that I would come back the next day.

"Many days throughout my journey I went without food. Older Brother, through all my suffering, I came to know this one, this great pain; understanding,

understanding that I, too, must have brought great pain to your life since childhood, always being my caretaker in everything, providing and protecting me on my every need. Older Brother, this understanding came by the way of great suffering, and not before. Brother, with all these different families I wasn't known to them as Younger Brother, but a slave with low understanding but great integrity for work. Out of all the land with family in it, I had one companion, a slave, not one equal to me in these burdens, because I was lesser than he was. He was a slave to one family, and I was a slave to many families, doing their will to survive from day to day. Older Brother, can you, will you find forgiveness for me?"

"Brother, once again I find foolishness in what you ask. Forgiveness? You are my brother, not some distant stranger in need of such things of which you ask. I, the older, have rejected the idea of you, my brother, being a slave, and those that had put this burden upon you will surely reap the things that they have sown, and they too will be made to accept the idea that you will be their King in all the things. I have heard in anger; by no means will all these districts and regions go unpunished, these very families will hate the day that you were their slave, so as of now let these families recline in their very ways, not even aware of what lies ahead for them. But for the one who was your companion, he will not suffer such things, but he will be of service to his Kings. Younger Brother, I ask you, do you take liking to this companion, and is he someone who can be trusted with different things?"

In reply, the Younger Brother said, "I do, Older Brother. In my time of despair, this very slave helped me escape, and that is the very reason why I am here with you this very day. It was him that told me to escape to the wilderness, because they dare not come to this place."

So the Older Brother asked, "Why this place?"

"Because of fear. Hunters of that region have reported and told of this beast that is a serpent, but eat men alive. These stories are known to all the families. When the hunters tell these stories, they tell it with fear in their eyes. These hunters have been a witness to this act, hunters who are alive while others escape with their very lives."

With the understanding of what the Younger Brother was saying, the Older Brother began to laugh.

Now the Younger Brother asked, "Brother, why do you laugh?"

"Because, Younger Brother, of my very gift. A souvenir that will be shared by me with others."

Not taking an understanding of what the Older Brother meant, the Younger Brother still joined the Older Brother in laughter. As dark began to set in, the brothers secured their place to stay with another fire.

"Now," the Older Brother says, "Younger Brother, let us feast again tonight. In fact, let us feast every night, until nothing is before our eyes."

The Older Brother had become delighted on the things the Younger Brother had enlightened him on; the fear that the families in different districts and region had of the man-eater.

As the night passed, the Older Brother and Younger Brother awoke from another night of celebration and unity at daybreak.

The Older Brother had gained his full strength and his sight back, saying, "Brother, I am at my full capacity in strength, sight, and mind now."

Interrupting before he could speak, the Younger Brother said, "Brother, should we abandon this place?"

The Older Brother said, "No Brother, let me speak without interruption. We are to stay here a little while longer, because all things have become known to me. Younger Brother, our absence apart has not been in vain, even though you suffered much. The time has come to be what we are to be; Kings. In everything you have told me, fate has played its role. Now, Younger Brother, lets us carry out the path that has been set forth for us. When I wasn't with you, during your time of humiliation and suffering, fate was watching over you as a witness while you endured all these things, necessary to be fitted as a King. Your exile to these families was much needed. Who or what else could have led you to me, in my time of need, saving my very life? I ask, who or what else, brother? This is further proof of us in our kingship."

Sitting there quietly as if he was in amazement of the things, his Older Brother continued, "Please keep silent, let me further myself in speaking; do not go blind to the things you have endured, nor go deaf to the things I say, because fate is no longer with you but I, the Older Brother, is, setting this stage for your performance as King, building its road for you to find me. Now we are together, where fate had ended, we will continue to raise you up from what has happened, but secure your thoughts in what will happen. Also, let's consider the slave that you were companion of; no suffering or harm will come to him, with all things taken into consideration. We will appoint him a position on our Kingdom to come, as the record keeper, writing about all our adventures to come. That which is at present and that which was in the past, keeping nothing from him, that which was in our darkest moment nor in our moment of light. Younger Brother, are you in agreement with appointing this slave this position?"

"Yes, Older Brother, I do. You have gathered well, in all I have told you, this is a well-fitted position for this slave of one family. Older Brother, even though I am ignorant to many things, as the Younger Brother you constantly show affectionate love for me, your Younger Brother. Discipline yourself to be reverent towards me and only me. Truly, you are your brother's keeper, in everything you have said and done. I have imprisoned all my hope in what you say will take place."

"Younger Brother, in this moment and our Kingdom to come, Brother, there are no more things for me to speak on, in such a matter that anyone that could hear of this wouldn't believe in it. Things that took notice of me and possessed me in their very ways. One encounter after another encounter. It all started when I fell in a deep sleep after we had departed from each other. During a long day of conversing with you, I began to dream, and in these dreams, I was approached by a man-shaped form who always kept his face concealed from me. Never knowing his identity, but knowing my interest at hand."

The Younger Brother asked, "Older Brother, could it be someone you have met in the past, exposing yourself in what our journey to rulership was to be, knowing you were doing this?"

Quickly the Older Brother spoke out loudly, saying, "No, never, not to any one soul, this man with the concealed face was an ally in my dreams, instructing me in different things, making my thoughts clear on what must be done on this road to Kingship, counseling me throughout my fleshly wants and desires. But I made it known to him that as long as my Younger Brother was with me, as my co-ruler. After dreaming, I held fast in what was being said and what I was saying, taking in all knowledge. But brother, behold on what will happen next, unaware, something that will exceed all of mankind's expectation of any race or authority. An introduction from a different source, making me knowledgeable and powerful. When working together, they are called the Different Ones, but in separation they made themselves know to me as the Thief, the Liar, the Adulteress, and the Murderer. Each one had a gift, making it only known to me, because I was appointed by them to carry out what we will be; Kings. One by one, freely, they made their case to me by means of action and words, but out of the four, the Murderer was the most dominant one. His authority was in every act, leaving no room for reasoning, but only for what must be done. Putting everything in its perspective place as he sees fit. None dare to challenge his authority. If they do so, they will be sent to non-existence and held by their own tombstone, not to be memorialized by family and friends. Fear was their master, and the Murderer was fear's master.

"Spreading through me like a disease, not to kill me but to preserve me so I can spread it like a plague against any that might be of objection to me being a King and you as a co-ruler. Then there was the Thief, who persuaded them from their belief in hope by asking the question, '*Who has hope, and in return what did hope bring?*' Pointing to the dead, saying, '*Have not many died for this hopeless hope? Now look, look.*' Who followed was the Liar. Deception was his way, reading it through stories as if it were the truth. Now who would stand firm, or who would surrender to his betrayal. All have fallen victim by his system of things.

"But look, behold this one, painting and concluding herself as the beginning and the ending of love, being blind by her intentions, unable to look past her beauty and the pleasurable things she does. All men have become deaf to any outside advice that was given and will not see the act of worship they give to her by carrying out whatever she wants. Who can control her, when being in opposition to her is a failed effort? I tell you, none except one, the Murderer, because this one is the head of them all, having no natural affection for beauty or anything else, only destruction for who or whatever opposes him. He watched in the shadows, allowing the others, the Different Ones, to approach me, only because he wanted them to reveal and teach me their ways. It was necessary to go out, through the different districts and regions, as something other than his gift to me, who would be King over all, if we only went out in his way as murderers.

"Now Younger Brother, as far as laws, we shall command that every man, woman, and child of the age of twelve and up will be iron-branded with our marking, showing that they are our people and we are their Kings. Those under the required age will be in their parents' care until they reach the age of the branded marking. No longer will they be in their parents' care but the property of the

King's. First, Younger Brother, this is the marking they shall wear from twelve until all the days of their life."

1

This is the representation of the long mass distance of land we are Kings over.

2

This is the representation of wide mass of land are Kings over.

3

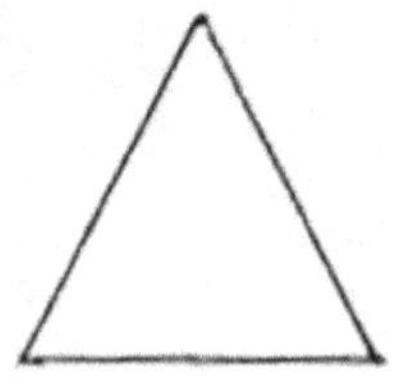

This is the representation of mountains, abode, hills, and valleys that we are Kings over.

4

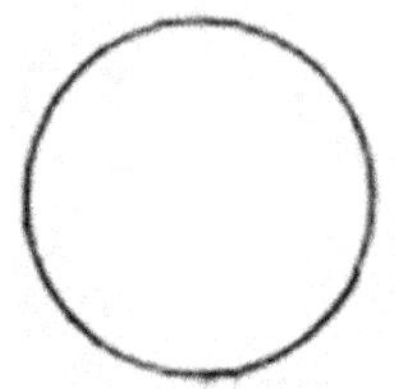

This is the representation of the circle of families foreign or domestic that we are Kings over. An inter-chain of families that lives on the long mass distance of land the wide mass distance of land, whether in the mountains, abode, hills, or valleys; we as Kings are their owner.

5

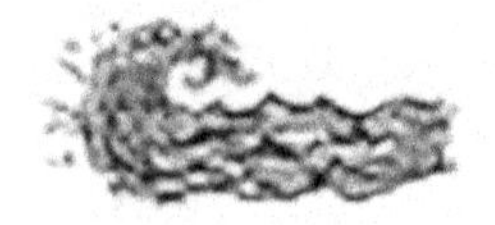

This is the representation of water that the Kings own where families are to drink from, also water the fields, livestock, and transportation of things from one place to another.

6

This is the representation of ownership—the symbol of the Brothers who are Kings.

1. Each and every person of age will be iron branded of all King's marking
2. All souls will continue to the Kingdom by ways of the very sweat off the flesh
3. Do not be found guilty of being in service to something other than your Kings
4. Let each person be found in his own district or region, not district mixing with region or region with district, nor should region be with other regions or district with other districts. Now, Younger Brother, we will approve men of their respective region or district to officiate our laws, and made sure that each law is carried out, and we will also make the living conditions of those who are appointed by the Kings better than normal, but not equal to a prince or greater than the Kings, showing that we can be generous Kings, ones that could be merciful if they make the laws a way of life. If any man rejects a law that has been approved by the Kings, severe punishment will immediately come up on him. A pledge of allegiance to the

Kingdom must be found in their work, on everything that the Kings will say or order.

"Also, Younger Brother, part of the responsibility of those who are officiating on behalf of the Kings is to ensure that the laws are to be visible in all the slave places of dwelling, the law that should be close enough to watch with your eyes and deep in the one that says, Do not be found guilty as a service to something other than your Kings. That law is the most important of the laws, the only thing that is greater than this law is what was announced in the beginning; if any law is to be changed, it will only be changed by the hands of the Kings. Also, let us not be ignorant in watching the mixing of district with region or region with region. Do not let it be known to the men that are officiating the Kings laws that we, as Kings, will approve other men on different accounts. They will impose, as slaves, among the people, making sure that the officers of the King are not organizing to bring this Kingdom to ruins by not practicing what is best in the interest of the Kings and the Kingdom. By self-appointing themselves as the way, speaking absolutely about this Kingdom's judicial decisions making it ours and only ours to make way to whomever do so and their seed.

"Mercy itself has no place for them now, Younger Brother. What was revealed to me has been revealed to you, in showing this to you, a secret that is so sacred, only for us. It is yet another example of the trust and love that I have for my Younger Brother, because this too will come to pass. So now, Younger Brother, at this moment, exhort yourself as King and nothing less."

After all things had been said by the Older Brother, the Younger Brother began to speak and say once again, "Older Brother, you have amazed the ears and mind, only to capture the heart throughout eternity. I will follow you as a co-ruler. There is one final question that I must ask, Older Brother, only to see clear; have the ones that you call the Different Ones cursed you into a game of wickedness and power?"

"No, Younger Brother, but challenged and tested. It is by virtue that we are to be seated as Kings. Now quiet yourself and rest well, tomorrow we will rise and carry out our duties as King, and our very first act is to find the slave that is in despair, who found courage in himself to help you escape."

Now at this time late evening was approaching and the Older Brother had rested himself, telling his Younger Brother all that will take place. Likewise, the Younger Brother rested himself from listening and inquiring things of his Older Brother. Both declined into meditation of different events to come, and how the next day was the beginning of those things to take place. They rested through the night until morning come, waking them up from their sleep.

Greeting each other as Kings, the Younger Brother said to the Older Brother, "Let us journey to the district of the slave, the slave of one family, one who was a true companion during a time of suffering of the body and thoughts.

"When I was at my falling point in failure, it was him that helped me cope with things that were heavy burdens for me, never speaking to the one that enslaved us about how it was him whose hands were on my assigned duties. Older Brother, you are to be commended many times over in making this slave an appointed position in our Kingdom."

"Younger Brother, commend me not, he has rightfully earned his position through you and by you in our Kingdom. But before we journey, let us gather water and food and anything of importance of us, because the next district you speak of is days of travel."

While in travel, the Younger Brother didn't hold fast in telling the Older Brother about things that they would face in the district where this slave was.

"In the district, Older Brother, we are sure to encounter opposition, because there I was a slave. Now the owners of me have marked me as escaped, punishable by death by my owners there. They also speak highly of the hunters there. They say, 'Is there anything, man or beast, that this district hasn't captured or will capture?' Who can say anything different, because many districts and regions have labeled them as this, too. Those same districts and regions have also come to them for certain hunts. They are known to many as master hunter, having displays of great things that have been killed or captured by their very hands. In their district the chieftain of the hunters in the one with the most captures or kills, or even the greatest hunt of them all. This is part of their tradition.

"I was often reminded by their chieftain hunter that I would be a waste for him to hunt, maybe a challenge for the beginners who hunt. Also, Older Brother, they are very crafty and skilled with iron, silver, bronze, and gold, shaping these very things into whatever they desire."

So the Older Brother began to say, "Younger Brother, all these things you speak I have taken into consideration. Because they are master hunters and skilled workers, and known throughout regions. We are their Kings, so to keep from desolating their very existence, I will offer them their very lives by saying, '*We as your Kings will offer you life as a slave, or death by pain. Choose, because I have ordered you a great burden, as you did my Younger Brother. There is no other offer.*'

Now night had approach them, but instead of entering the district this night they camped on the outer part of the district, waiting, resting, and sleeping until the dawn of morning. As dawn began to break into the early morning, the Older Brother and the Younger Brother awoke from their sleep and rose, gathering their supplies.

Because the district was in sight, the Older Brother turned and looked at his brother, saying, "Do not fear. It is those who are not my brother who should fear. We will reach their camp of their district in the tenth hour of the morning now."

The Younger Brother began to say, "I have never feared with you my Older Brother by my side."

As they came nearer and in sight of the camp, the Younger Brother became recognized. Talk spread throughout the camp saying that the escaped slave had returned, but with a different look. One with a look of vengeance, and the one that accompanied him also carried that look. Had they come without their sense, and guided by senselessness?

Never, in any generation of their people, had a slave escaped, but what was more disturbing was for one to escape and then come back. Had he come back to mock the people?

The families he slaved for, but most importantly the master hunters, did not know the one who accompanied him or what was about to occur to them, not even a just cause would save them. This was a crime punishable by death. As the brothers journeyed through the district, finding themselves center-ways of the district, they were met by the chieftain and all his assemblies, made up of master hunters and the families the Younger Brother slaved for. A sum of 950 master hunters and a sum of 550 families, a total of 1500, assembled against the brothers, who came face to face with this assembly.

The chieftain began speaking, saying, "Slave, did you escape to bring shame upon our district, that is known throughout many districts and regions as master hunters? Only to bring another slave with you, and who is this slave? The one who will take your place, after you receive your punishment of death by this district?"

Before the Younger Brother would answer, the Older Brother said, "Are you the chieftain of the master hunters? And are these the families that the one you call 'slave' slaved for?"

With the numbers of the assembled in his favor, he responded, "I am the chieftain of the master hunters, and yes, these were and still are the families that were his masters."

"Then let me say, I am called the Older Brother, and the one you call 'slave' is called the Younger Brother, my only flesh. We have traveled a great distance to offer you, the families and the master hunters, a gift and practice of tradition that you have as law."

Now, kneeling to the things they had gathered, the Older Brother said this as he began to uncover a souvenir for all who were present: the head of the giant man-eater. Immediate fear struck all who were present, paralyzed in movement.

The Younger Brother said, "Now, to honor the tradition of law in this district." He kneeled down to the left of his brother.

All who were present reached into their belongings, coming out with sharp weapons, like the one his Older Brother used to kill the giant serpent. He rose up from his kneeling position, only to behead the chieftain of the master hunters on this day.

"Let it be known that your law was fulfilled and the greatest hunt ever of this district, or any other district or region has fallen before the brothers." As the Younger Brother continued speaking, he said, "but yet we offer one last gift to the ones who assemble against me and my brother, and all the people of this district; life as slaves or a tombstone. Because you have treated your tradition as law concerning the chieftain, who is chosen by way of most captured or the greatest kill, the brothers are declaring this tradition lawless because we have surpassed any hunts. We shouldn't be called upon as your chieftains, but your Kings. Anything other than this is punishable. '*Kings,*' you will say, '*Kings,*' you must say."

"I as your Older King will appoint from among you men that will serve as officers to the Kings in your old tradition. Men who are skilled in hunting, you called them master hunters. It is these men among you who I will choose as officer of the Kings, and the rest will stay with you as master hunters. Now, concerning the laws of your Kings, you shall keep and preserve them, passing it down from generations, making it a way of life."

At hearing this, the people of this district, along with the families and the master hunters, began to fill with distress, agonized with the burden that had befallen them all. Weeping, asking themselves, 'who are these brothers who have become Kings over us? In our own errors to his brother, we must suffer, taking out customs, traditions, and laws, making them lawless to him and in the eyes of our people, and our children.'

Now one person asked from the crowd of people, saying, "Why should a district of people suffer so much of one man?"

In reply, the Older King said, "Why did so many people in a district didn't show any compassion for one man?"

This silenced the one who asked, bringing shame to such a question.

"Let every master hunter the ages of 55 and up station themselves before me."

The sum of the master hunters 55 and up was 50. As they made themselves in front of the Kings, the King said, "These men of your district, of your people, who were called master hunters will proclaim that they are officers to the Kings, not master hunters, because I have appointed them as the Kings' officers. Now, doing it publicly, making these men take an oath of fulfilling the obligation that was about to be put upon them. From the least to the greatest in age. You men with the greatest age will be the senior officers of the officers. While carrying his responsibility, he is also responsible for making sure that you carry out your obligation without failing. It is not permitted for a lower ranking officer to have authority over his senior officer. Everything he says, you must do, because his orders come from the Kings themselves. Any attempt to do otherwise is punishable by the Kings.

"Each officer of the King is responsible for a family. For each 50 families to 50 officers, the senior officer will divide the master hunters and the people of this district to an officer of the Kings."

Because this district was great in numbers, 14 days passed before the senior officer's task was complete. During this time, the Kings stayed with the enemy they hated so much; the families. They kept their anger from blazing against the families, because there was something much greater at hand; the Kingdom.

The families were the ones known to have gold and power, more than anyone in all districts or regions, except for the master hunters. They depended on the master hunters for food and control of anything that might get out of hand. In the staying of the families, the Kings had covered 28 families, leaving the 22 most powerful families for last. Now, the most powerful families proved to be in union about not having the brothers as Kings over their district, because the riches and power was still at their will and not of the Kings'.

In hearing this, the Kings said to their ranking officer, "Meet with the master hunters, and in the meeting among the Kings officer and the master hunter you must tell them to speak with the last of the families, saying that all their customs and laws are no more, only what the Kings say is law and order."

At saying this, the Kings knew that it would provoke the last of the families even more. Just as the Kings ordered the ranking officer to do, they did, and the ranking officer spoke by means of the Kings. At hearing what was said, the 22 families grew angry and began to speak abusively about the Kings, just as the Kings knew, denouncing them as Kings. At hearing this, the Kings acted quickly, telling their senior officer that this was grounds for punishing.

The last of the families, as the Kings saw fit, furthered themselves in talk with the senior officer and the master hunters, bringing the last and most powerful 22 families into custody. They were charged them with denouncing the Kings, and all they said. They had the master hunters stand guard at each and every entrance and exit of the families' dwelling place, keeping any and all intruders out.

"Protecting the very riches they possess, only the ones that will wear or have a special piece you will show, and you will see with your very eyes this special piece," said the Older Brother.

In ending the talk with the senior officer, they did just as the Kings commanded. Joining the master hunters and telling them what had been said. They immediately went out in gathering and brought the last most powerful families into custody. Once they had all the families, they were told what they had been charged with, and that they were to go in front of the Kings to see what punishment must be carried out against them.

But before the Kings could carry out any punishment, they had to do according to what they had said, or they themselves as Kings would be looked upon as Kings that had defrauded themselves as being Kings.

The Younger Brother said to the Older Brother, "Let us not defraud ourselves of what we are. Let me make fellowship with the senior officer, saying, 'find the workmen in this district that can craft iron, metal, gold, silver, wood, and stones into whatever the Kings may desire. While you, Older Brother, hold the families into custody until you decide what punishment must be executed on them so that I may finish this task of commanding the senior officer on what to do."

Feeling relieved because of what the Younger Brother had said, the Older Brother went to the midst of the senior officers, telling them in a commanding way what they must do. "Failing is not tolerable by the Kings, nor is disappointing them on anything they say. Go from me, bring me the men that work with their hands in iron, metal, gold, silver, wood, and stone."

As they departed from the Kings, the Kings held fast to the families by imprisoning them from all other things. As two days passed, nothing was heard from the senior officers, but on the third day, as was told to the younger King, the officer was standing with the men that the younger King had asked for.

Now making it clear to the men, he said, "I am one of two of your Kings, the Younger King, and my brother is your Older King, not yet present because he is attending other matters. But I have had my senior officers to gather you in order for you to be of service to your Kings. I am ordering you to have a special piece made for my senior officer. This piece will represent that they are officers of the

Kings, and not to be ordered or take commands by anyone other than their Kings. Now, these are your instructions on how this special piece must be made. It will be made of gold, with a symbol of our likeness on it, and also with their names engraved on it. This special piece must be worn at all times, and this is how it will be made. 1: the circle is a symbol of a circle, that only surrounds the Kings. 2: the crown with his name and number on it is a representation of the King's officers. 3: the gold is a representation of worth appointed by the Kings.

"This special piece will not confuse those who will come in the name of the Kings, and expose those who speak with fraudulence that they are the King's officers. Now, the higher-ranking officer to the lowest ranking officer will wear this special piece to with a number beside their names, signifying rank."

He asked the men, the workmen who crafted in gold, silver, wood, iron, metal, and stone, "What years of experience do you have in this craft?"

They spoke in order, telling the Young King what years of experience they had with this craft. After all had been said, the Young King chose the man with the most experience for something different, a different assignment. He was ordered to be the Kings' top craftsman in and on their assignment, and as the Kings' top craftsman he was ordered to hand-make two crowns for the Younger King and the Older King. Also, he was to make the sharp object that had killed the man-eating serpent into a weapon.

"That is desired by the Kings. Now let the officers lead the craftsmen back to the family place that they had occupied as their dwelling place, only to collect those things that value in gold, silver, wood, iron, metal, and stone. Once this thing which I am commanding you to make is complete, report back to your King. This is one of many things to come in proving your loyalty to your Kings. While not in the presence of your King, if anything may come about with disturbance or disorderly, you workmen will bring this matter to the King's officer, and if the King's officer fails to resolve this matter, then this matter must be a concern for the Kings' highest-ranking officer.

"If this matter continues, then the highest-ranking officer must appoint to lowest ranking officer to bring this matter to the Younger King, and they must tell all that concern this matter so he can determine how to remove any and all obstacles that have arisen."

As the Young King dismissed himself, one final thing was said to his officer; "Follow all my instructions to the fullest or you yourself will be denied as the Kings officer, and live as a slave instead of a personal servant, as an officer of the Kings. Nor will there be any mercy upon you, because of what you were rather than what you will become by not carrying out the instructions you have been instructed to do."

As the officers of the Kings were leading the workmen back to the abode or dwelling place of the families, and the Young King went back in the direction of his brother, they were met by the unexpected; the slaves and workers of the families. Not being far from sight the Young King, a short distance away, had stopped to see what outcome would take place.

As the approach had come to an end with all slaves and workers standing in midst of the officers, they began to speak, saying, "We are the workers and slaves of the families that have returned to the families, because we have no supplies. No food and water to continue in our laborious, everyday work. These concerns have led us back on our way so we, the slaves and workers, may continue in our daily work. Without these supplies, the slaves and the workers will surely die. Because you all are known to me, but I as a slave to one family am, not known to you. May I ask the master hunters, are you all headed in this direction to correct these concerns with the families?"

At hearing this, the Young King recognized the voice of the person speaking, so the Young King turned from the direction of his Older Brother to go back in the midst of his officers, the slaves, and the workers only to see if his hearing had deceived him. Once he was in the midst of all of them, not only had his hearing not deceived him, but also his eyes were a witness to the companion that he wanted to find alive dearly.

The Young King began to speak, saying, "I am your King, me and my Older Brother, and the one you called master hunter are not this anymore, but the very ones you see and didn't accompany you in your journey. They are mine and my Older Brother's officers, and the families you look for are no more."

Not in looks but by voice, he, too, was recognized. Now he stumbled with words, not even able to speak but only able to point.

"You will not serve the families, but your Kings only, and not continue your life as a slave or worker. If any choose not to listen but see the things in the former way of the families, not abiding by the laws, a command that has been passed down to the officers, which will be passed down to you, then you are not fitted to be a slave nor a worker, but to reside in a tombstone."

Now as he silenced himself with talk, but walked and confronted the man who was the spokesperson for the slaves and workers, saying, "You, you were a companion, a loyal friend to me in my times of need. Your time has come to be no man's slave. I am saying this so all can hear; not families, nor anyone from my lowest ranking officer to my highest-ranking officer will have command over you. Only the Kings. Your needs and wants will be met, because you have rightfully owned this position, this level of royalties in our Kingdom to come. As for the rest of you slaves and workers, that is your position to own until your death, so follow my officer and do as you are commanded by them."

In closing of his talk, the Young King greeted his old companion with a hug. "So, old companion, let us be reacquainted with not what was, but what is going to be. Let us do it in walking in the direction of your Older King, but my Older Brother."

Now able to speak, the slave to one family said, "Old companion that has become my King, first I ask for your forgiveness for not being able to speak, but in my surprise, I was unable to speak."

"This is forgivable," said the Young King.

"Young King, I ask for one other forgiveness. Forgive me, because I thought your existence was no more. I grieved many days and nights, thinking that had I not done enough to prepare you for your escape, because at that time you were fragile to so many things, and had your journey swallowed you, alive and unable to defend yourself."

"This too is forgivable, because these things were meant to happen. There's one other thing; I will grant to you anything you ask other than the things I have told you with now or later. Do we have this understanding?"

In answering, the slave to one family said, "We do, my King."

"Everything that took place during my time of distress, my other brother knows of. Of every deed you did for me, at hearing them, my Older Brother, your Older King, allowed me to appoint you a position in our Kingdom to come by means of me. You will be a record keeper of the Kings, but known to people as the Book Keeper."

As the Young King and the now Book Keeper of the Kings were on the road heading back to the district of his Older Brother, they were met by a messenger of the older King, saying, "Young King, I have an urgent message for you and only you. I have been instructed to hand deliver this message only to you."

At hearing this, the Young King said, "Do tell quickly, messenger."

While still prostrating himself, he said, "Young King, not for my eyes but for your eyes only."

Now, at hearing this, the Young King knew that this was a messenger that could be trusted, because telling the message 'do tell' was only a test by the Young King to see if the messenger eyes had been on the message that was meant for the Young King, as the message was delivered in writing.

It read, 'Young Brother, in your time away I have begun to establish our Kingdom to come by eliminating the families that were in my custody. These very ones hated our laws and were chanting that we restore their old laws and customs. To this very chant I took offense, to me and my Young Brother as Kings, so I took the very thing that they were accustomed to and put them to death, using the ones that they thought were their relief was their death; the master hunters. I persuaded them, saying "*who's next, who is to be an officer of the Kings, having authority over many by means of the Kings, who shall lift themselves up from a master hunter to an officer of the Kings, not only in this district but all district and regions? Prove yourselves by eliminating all the families that oppose the new law and the Kings.*" Without fail, the master hunters eliminated all the families without me myself having to do it all by myself. Now the very hills that look over this district are the tombstones of the families, with a sign saying, "they opposed." Now, Younger Brother, I hope you find even more courage in standing as a King, because of this very thing that has taken place, in this district, to have fear and order of our law. What you say in this district will not be challenged by the people here. It is waiting on your very arrival, whether by day or night. But as for myself and some of the master hunters that I have appointed as officers, we are traveling to neighboring districts and regions to eliminate any and all that opposes us as Kings. Even though distant lands we must travel, I, as the Elder Brother will always keep you informed as to my whereabouts through a messenger, and he must know the secret passwords of a messenger, which is "*troubling past of the Kings*." Young Brother, I was careful in choosing these very words, and these words were chosen because of what was troubling in every land will soon be (Kings'), a brief detail of me and you.

'Also, Young Brother, I request that when the time is right in your eyes, you give the officers the dwelling place of the families, because this has and will be fit for our very purpose. I also must add, because our Kingdom is to come, do not rest yourself as a permanent resident but become a foreigner in neighboring land and distant land, as a King in secret, but in the eyes of the people, an alien that resides as a common man. In this district that I am leaving but yourself are coming into, direct yourself. I shall take and direct myself in the north and east of this district that I am leaving, but you, Younger Brother, should direct yourself in the south and west of every district and region. You should come into this and will certainly see that we will cover all land. Be careful and not careless in everything you do, and say nothing to expose yourself as a King. To be revealed as King in other district or region will bring defiant disorder, an uprising that could result in death for you, a King.

'This is what is to be done in other districts and regions that neighbor the district you are coming into. Do not go into other districts or regions with many men, nor should they come in as officers, but disguise themselves as a wanderer, seemingly as no threat to the district or region, even though they are officers of the Kings acting as wanderers to spy the place out, learning their ways, culture, and laws only to destroy it. Come weeks apart and bring 12 with you, bringing no suspicions to themselves. In this way, do this in districts and regional lands that are far and distant, but for the district regions that are neighboring to the district in which you are, reenter using 12 common men, commanding them in all they must do while having their loved ones in custody. Say, "do this, do that, for the sake of your love ones." In doing this, Younger Brother, our officers, who they called master hunters, will not come to be recognized in the neighboring districts and regions, because they are all known and well depended on for the great hunts. Now, in ending this letter, let me say this; blood and tears will be shared, not love and peace, until our Kingdom come.'

After reading all that needed to be read and not replying in a form of a letter, the Young King said, "Is there no end to my Older Brother's wisdom? And yet, have knowledge while both the record keeper and the messenger are present."

In addition to that, the Young Brother said, "Messenger, tell my Older Brother, your Eldest King, '*troubling past of the Kings.*'"

At hearing what the Young King had said, the messenger left, deporting back to his Eldest King, saying, "My King, I do report back to you from your Younger Brother, my Young King, not with a letter but with these words: *troubling past of the Kings.*"

This was evidence that the letter he sent and the words that were returned back to him had been delivered. Now the Older King asked the messenger, "In what way does my Younger Brother travel?"

The messenger replied and said, "The Young King travels the road back to the district which we have left."

Now this was more good news to Older Brother. "Because you have both went and came for your Older King and your Younger King, you yourself will be just that; a messenger carrying letters or words back and forth between your Kings traveling wherever I may go. Messenger, do you have a family?"

In response, the messenger said, "My King, I myself have no family, it is only me."

So the Older King said, "As a gift from me, take three days for yourself and return to me as my messenger. It is here I will station myself along with my officers, waiting upon your return.

Gladly, the messenger accepted what the Older King had said. Meanwhile, the Young King and the record keeper were a day off from re-entering the district that he and his Older Brother had.

Once again together during the rest of that day of long travel, the Young King had become silent, but the record keeper didn't ask the Young King what had silenced him.

In thoughts, the record keeper said to himself, "Was it the letter that had silenced the Young King?"

Time had passed throughout the day and the Young King and the record keeper had come to the entrance of the district, and now entered into the entrance of the district. The Young King and the record keeper were both welcomed, but it wasn't by love, but through fear that they were welcomed and greeted. Once inside, there had been made for them an established place of rest.

Now at rest, the Young King said to the record keeper, "Because you did not press your King in asking question but waited on this time, the time that now your King will break his silence freely, I will say that in the letter and time before the letter there was words spoken in which I have and will share with you about our journey and destiny. This letter only furthers me in what must be done in satisfying any thoughts that may arise.

"Know every word will be carried out like a promise or an oath, so go out and find material in which you must write. And you must write every word that I have and will express to you, without any words in return."

The record keeper did just that, writing every word of the King's journey, not adding any words of his own. Days, weeks, and even months had come and went while spending this necessary time with Young King, having servants and caretakers at his demands.

Now, six months had passed when one of his lower ranking officer came in front of the Young King, greeting the Young King with a kiss as he bowed down in front of him, saying, "Young King, I have been requested to come to you about all matters concerning your demand by the high ranking officer."

At looking upon the lower ranking officer before he could speak, the Young King began to notice his garment and the special piece of gold he wore. The one he gave specific order to make. In seeing this, the Young King said to the lower ranking officer, "Now, are you here to tell me that all things that were commanded by me are complete?

"Yes, my King, and to show more obedience to the Kings the high-ranking officers have also ordered women to hand weave the finest linen for your officers and the Kings themselves, but only by the approval of the King. I have with me garments for the King and of the officers. Shall I present these garments?"

They were laid out in front of the King, and the King took a liking to what he saw. "So tell me, why have the high-ranking officers gone beyond what was ordered for them to do?"

"I, myself, along with lower ranking officer and the high-ranking officer, maybe thought that the King himself would remember and keep us as ranking official and not be put to death without telling the lower ranking officer that he took a liking to the garments."

He said, "Leave the garments, but as for you, you must leave at once, tell the lower ranking officer to the highest-ranking officer I will meet with them in seven days."

Turning to the record keeper, he said, "How do you, as the King's closest acquaintance, see what has transpired in the high-ranking officers' decision to go beyond what was ordered? Making way in trying to soften the King in order to keep their position?"

"I well know, as should my King, this is no conspiracy against the Young King and your Older Brother, my Eldest King. Who are they who would dare trade death for the things of which the King have and will give?" These very words that were spoken by the record keeper were accepted and cherished by his King.

Now as for the Elder King, those three days came and went with both keeping the words that were said, moving throughout different regions and districts as stated by the Eldest King. Just as those three days came and went for the Older King, so did the seven days with the Younger King. But before the seven days, as the Young King had said, he spoke all the things that were in the letter the Older Brother had written to the record keeper, continuing his writing and everything that was said before and at that moment. As day seven arrived, the Young King went out and met with them all, men that crafted with their hands gold, silver, wood, iron, metal, stones. Even the top craftsman that was to make the crown for the young and Older King, also the lower officers to the high-ranking officers were all stationed in front of him.

Seeing with his own eyes the completion of everything he had commanded, the Young King said, "Befriend the laws and keep the laws as a savior of your life, and always honor me and my brother as your Kings. There is one last command you must honor, and you will honor this command; in the district I just left in order to meet with you all, then only when this is done, will the King and his Older Brother, your Elder King, honor you as their officials that will not perish from their positions. Everything that me or my brother has commanded or put in place as law you must do."

They followed and put in practice all that was said, from their branding from age 12, to making slaves, to carving images of the laws, and even death itself. They, the officers, didn't leave anything out. As for the Young King, he was pleased because the district was so big in size that it took nine months before all could be delivered. After the nine months, the King summoned his appointed officer for a meeting.

"Now hear this, because in every effort you have made for your Kings in bringing all my commands true, and going beyond that, was order. I have accepted this, and you have proved yourself to always be an officer of the King. In return for your service to the Kings and their Kingdom to come, it is I that will reward my officer with a gift. This is the second highest honor to receive from your Kings because the first is being appointed an officer of the Kings and not choosing your ways over your Kings' ways. As an officer of the Kings, an officer must be established and established he will be. That's why I am giving you, my officer, a dwelling place and their wealth and riches of the families to my officers.

"Let the wealthiest families' dwelling place, land, and riches go to my highest-ranking officer, and the rest of the families' dwelling places, land, and riches go to my lower ranking officers, because no officer, high in rank or low in rank, none have authority over the King's friend and record keeper. In knowing this, he will have first choice of the family dwelling place, land, and wealth.

Because emotion was high after what the King had done, the lowest ranking officer spoke, saying, "With all that has happened, is it this day that should wash away everything that has happened to our people, our culture, our laws. Inflicting such pain as that will always be memorable." Before he could speak another word, a certain officer put him to death.

To keep the King's anger from blazing, all other officers accepted the Kings' gift while screaming in one accord, "We accept."

The King's heart was one of reasoning, to make sure the King's anger wouldn't blaze. They presented something that the Kings' eyes had not been set on. The weapon that had killed the man-eating serpent.

It had been hammered and melted into, not one, but two swords. That was something more liked than the fine linen that was woven by the women. But what was to be handed to him next was more than just a gift, it was the fulfillment of what the brothers were to be: Kings. The crowns. In doing this, they didn't fail, because the Kings' anger didn't blaze. In fact, the King was pleased. During the time that the King was being pleased, all officers were pleased and happy because everything the King had commanded was accomplished, meaning there was no sign that the King would take their lives or position now, because the King was struck with being pleased.

He had once sent a messenger out with the letter telling all what was said and did with the secret password, *"troubling past of the Kings."* Also, the Younger Brother reminded the Older Brother that he would be doing exactly what was told to him, residing in lands near and far as a common man, an alien.

Turning to his record keeper, he said, "Because now is the moment that things are made good, and I am pleased with everything that has taken place, this is and must be the moment I must leave."

And so he did, but not before having met with the highest and lowest ranking officer, telling them that he and his Older Brother have put forth laws and commands that they must uphold.

"If not, it is punishable by death, and I, your Younger King, will leave the record keeper in charge of all matters. So now go. Go from me and be the Kings' officer, but talk with your King as his record keeper. Bring with you 12 of the lowest ranking officers."

And so he did. As they walked, the King told them what task was at hand and all they must do. "When you have completed this task with your King, you will come back to this district that we are leaving and inherit all that your

Kings have said. The dwelling places, the land, and the riches of the families."

As they were reaching the outer edge of the district they were leaving, the Young King said to the record keeper, "See all that goes well with the laws, commands, and everything that I have promised my officers."

Making his promise that he would, the record keeper turned back, going in the direction of the district they were leaving.

The King said, "Record keeper, I will write to you of any or all matters that is of importance, or just to keep you informed."

As the record keeper reached the heart of the district, he immediately started putting things in order of what the Young King had spoken of.

Now, throughout different districts, regions, and lands where the Young King and the Older King traveled, they put to the rest the laws, tradition, and customary ways of doing things, little by little destroying any and everything that they believed in and replacing it with their laws, becoming Kings and appointing officers of that particular place and land.

But in the land in which the Young King was going, he was about to come face to face with something that was unexpected, and he himself questioned these feelings he was having, and also what he saw and what he was having, and also ask what he saw and what he saw struck him.

Not able to keep his sense or to withdraw from his talk, he approached what he had seen, saying, "Woman, is it possible for a man and a woman to create such beauty?"

In answering what the Young King had said, she said, "You come to me speaking on what you see—beauty. But let me speak on what is known. A woman, one who has been defiled in many ways by her own acts to survive and also forced by men to perform acts of prostitution or to work, for title, or food, or even a piece of clothing. Not in their dwelling place, they allow me to sleep, but I am free to lay anywhere near the place they dwell. Now, with an abusive tongue, they say, 'why should filth eat what I eat, sleeping in the place where I dwell, or wear clothing made of fine lining?' So sir, I say to you that beauty has cursed me only to be a slave to things that are defiled, only growing in old age or death itself will I only be free. Alone. I am in this alone, I face that my name itself has been taken from me, Angana, and replace by my own people in this land with 'Whore.'"

In hearing all what the woman had said, the Young King said, "Because you showed courage in telling me, a common man, the brutal truth, Angana, and didn't deceive me, your enemy will be my enemy and alone you will not be. I am taking you away, not to taunt you, but you will be called by your name, Angana."

Now she began to say, "If you can carry out the very words you speak, I, Angana, will put my life in your hand. Submissive I shall be in everything you ask all the days of my life."

"Now, Angana, take my hand and trust that I will do right by you all the days of your life. Leave with me, and let this way of living burden you no more."

Taking her hand, he led her from that place, only to put her in a remote place where that both stayed, keeping his ways as a common man. So she wouldn't know that he was a King. There he built an abode. By day, the King and his officers continued in their ways to destroy the laws, the traditions, and all the things that they carry out in this district. Provided and protected was Angana, but, disciplined, the King did not have relations with her, for he didn't want to bring more shame in what she was, but to preserve her for something more dreamy; a relationship that grows into a marriage. And this went on for a while, in fact, for months, until he finally took his position as King in this district. Once he became King, he brought Angana into what wasn't known by her; that he had become King in her district and that he was King in many districts and regions alongside with his brother.

"This I share with you, because you must live your life as my wife. A queen."

After being struck in her heart on what was being said, she accepted with tears of joy, saying, "Because you, my King, the people's King, have delivered me from great distress, I shall be more than a wife, but also a servant to the King, my husband."

Soon after all had been said, a marriage ceremony took place in the district in which she came from, but when they looked to see who the bride of the King was and saw, now they knew more than a bride was at hand, but revenge itself. They started to remember all the pain that they had caused to the queen.

Then the King began to make announcements concerning the queen and the district, saying, "A day, a day of both happiness and sadness. The happiness will be won by the King and his Queen Angana, but the sadness is owed to the people of this district, because of the ceremonies that will take place; one of the marriage and one of the death."

He commanded his officers to bring before him the men who mentally and physically abused the queen.

Queen Angana and the King himself knew every man that was her abuser, because she shared the very name of every man over a period of time while living remote.

As every man was brought before him and the queen, the King said, "You abusers, you have been living in security from your very acts, but today will prove different. Whoever stands with you or for you to secure you from me, call upon them and save yourself, because death is here for you and I, the King, will not keep it waiting for your very soul."

Now giving the order, the men were hanged by the King's officers and left there for three days until the marriage ceremony was over. Only then did the King allow the district to bury their dead, and it served as a memory of the King's powers.

Now as time was spent together as husband and wife, the King and Queen proved to be far and beyond everything that they could want in sharing what they had and felt for each other. An extended family member was born, a son, a prince. Calling him Phel'ra, the first born of the King and Queen in the height of their happiness.

The King wrote to his Older Brother, the King, and the record keeper, telling them all that had happened and also telling the record keeper he must leave and search throughout to see if anywhere measured up to him and his Elder Brother as King.

"The second in charge must take your place, and you must make him aware of all his duties and responsibilities as second in charge."

After recording all that had been told to him in his letter, the record keeper did just that and left his post to fill his King's request. After receiving his letter from the messenger with the secret passwords being spoken by the messenger, "*troubling past of the Kings,*" the Elder King knew this was from his Younger Brother sending the messenger.

On his way, the Older Brother began to read the letter, finding joy in his brother's letter and saying quietly to himself, "Because I and my Younger Brother have engaged in war with many districts and regions through destroying their laws, customs, and traditions, I too have found delight in my Younger Brother's joy; being a King, finding a wife, making her his Queen, Queen Angana, and last his son, my nephew—Prince Phel'ra. Also telling his Queen of his Older Brother, although my brother is distant, I too have begun to experience feelings for a woman of interest, Naveen. Naveen can only be explained as a woman of different circumstance, because she has not been damned by the hardship of life. Not since birth. Only a life of male and female servants, untouched by any man's touch, she was not to feel man's touch until she was married. Flesh of men of all sort came, wanting to leave with her, flesh they all left pure in flesh, pure in acts, even when she spoke her thoughts through her mouth, nothing that was damaging to one's heart. She softened the King's heart. A virgin to wrong-doing, I was a watchman in disbelief. I became a non-believer in who she was. How much more does this woman require? Then more I shall give her. With my own eyes I have seen Naveen turn down men of all sort with power and riches for her hand in marriage. Have I been wrong? Has this woman Naveen set herself above men that are privileged in power and riches, or have I misunderstood her reason for not marrying? It is for her that I have not yet desolated this district. The time has come for resolve. She must be tested and prove otherwise, because I, the King, have found myself in awe of her."

In seeing all that he saw, the King decided with reasoning to be a King with kind words. So the King approached Naveen and said, "Much has been seen, much has been done. Should a man die without love?"

In answering him, she said, "Only a man that knows what love is. He himself shouldn't die without it. Do you yourself know of it?"

In reply, he said, "Please excuse me, but I am known as Older Brother, a King in many districts and many regions."

In her reply, she said, "I am called Naveen."

So the King said, "Yes I do, only when a person thinks less of himself and more of the person at hand is when love is conceived. Never have I heard a King or a person in power speak as you do now." Becoming attentive in what he was saying, the King went on to say, "Now let me say and let it be heard, love is a practice in action, not just words. To say so, not one but both are a practitioner of love. This is the greatest power of all in any relationship, as hours become day, day turn into night, day and night replace weeks out of weeks, then there are months, then a year occur year after year only to behold years, years will age man and woman, only to be founded by death. This is how long you should practice love."

Now in tears, Naveen said, "Please speak no more, because you are a man worthy to be King. Who? Not even I would have known that a King knew the very thing that my heart yearns for, this endless love that you, as King, speaks of has captured my soul. Because my father has been a man of power and riches before I was born, always having male and female servants at my every call, giving me all my needs and wants. This love you offer have made these things not first in life. In my father's attempt to maintain my happiness, he failed only to leave me in search of it."

Now the King came into full understanding of Naveen. That, as a watchman, she was just as she appeared to be, for the men she turned away came offering more of the same and not what was really needed; a man that was an understanding man of true love, a petitioner.

So the King said, "End your search and begin your life of love with me, as my Queen."

"I, with a complete heart, accept being your Queen, but I have to do the honorable thing in telling my father."

"In doing this, you must tell your father you do this in reflection in his upbringing of you as his daughter, one who will respect all you are. What you have done and will do for me, but because you are a woman deeply founded on things of good facts, I ask you not to tell your father that I am King."

As she became disturbed at what the King had said, she said, "In not telling my father you are King, it is the King's request for me to lie to my father."

Now with a concerned look, the King said, "Naveen, my Queen, do no such thing. Do not lie to your father. Do not bring to his attention my title, but rather speak more on your love for me and my love for you. I am afraid if you speak on my title as King, your father will dismiss our love for each other and become vocal on my position and power, not seeing that it is my love for you that is more important than my Kingship. So please, because I do not want to lose you, be silent on this matter."

After making sense on what the King had said, Naveen decided not to risk what they had together: "love."

As she came into her father's presence, she began to flatter her father by saying, "Who have served me, a daughter, better than my father? A father among fathers, being all that a daughter or a son would want or need. A father you will always be, but the time has come for my father to have a son, one that is loved both by the father and his daughter."

"Naveen, are you asking for me to seed a son?"

In answering, Naveen said, "No, only in practice, because of who you are. I know you love me and want and expect nothing less than that for me. Many men have come, and we think that wanting my hand in marriage with the blessing of my father, but they all failed. None have been approved. This itself, in thoughts, made it difficult for my father, thinking he had failed, or his daughter was unable to love. All these thoughts have proved to be false if this wasn't true. I, Naveen, your daughter, would say so. Love, I have found the image of my father when it comes to wanting love for me. This man I have approved now, I'm asking for your blessing in marriage. A son you will gain, and a wife I will be."

Now, because her father loved her, he had no reason to doubt or to become suspicious of her. In his reply, her father said, "Naveen, because you as my daughter have always been obedient in all my teaching, and showing self-discipline towards what was bad, there is no reason not to believe you. If it's love you have found, then let this love bring this man forward to meet with me."

So, in that, she organized meeting after meeting. They met until Naveen's father took a liking to him. He himself found no reason they shouldn't be married. In all that he asked, and what was said in their constant meetings, there was no evidence of bad intent.

So, Naveen's father brought both of them in front of him, saying, "I do give you my blessing to marry my only child, my only daughter. Please let me, as the bride's father, make all the necessary arrangement for this marriage."

And so, they did, and so he did, and they were married. Soon after the marriage, Naveen became pregnant and birthed a boy, naming him Ker'cill. Love and peace were with the Older Brother, Naveen, and their son. As time went on, the Older Brother stayed steadfast in all his love for his wife and his son, even his father-in-law.

Naveen's father began to say, "What she had already seen, a son I have gained, and a wife she was to be to my son. Son, being a grandfather was a gift for me even at this time."

Naveen, his daughter, proved to be right once more. He himself began to see what she had seen, his image in his son-in-law who he thought of as a son, how he stayed true to his love for his wife and son.

At the same time, the Older Brother began to write his brother with a short message, saying, 'My brother, your brother has fathered a son and taken a wife, and all is well. Naveen is my wife. Ker'cill, my son, is now part of our family and because they are a part of me you should show nothing less than love for them as I do for your wife, your Queen, Queen Angana, your son, your prince, Prince Phel'ra."

After finishing his message in writing, he gave it to a messenger, one who came with him, but that was not known, saying, "You must deliver this to my brother, your King, and you must say to him, '*troubling past of the Kings.*'"

So just as the Older Brother command, the messenger did, because he knew to that the Older Brother was his King in the district in which he was dwelling. He delivered it.

Now relieving the messenger from his duty, the young King began to read, and found that he too was a brother-in-law and an uncle. He found great joy in what was said. In fact, so much joy that he began to tell his wife, the Queen, saying, "Angana, we have an extended family, because my brother took a wife and made her his Queen, Queen Naveen. They also had a son, Prince Ker'cill. This should be a day of celebrating, but instead we will all celebrate together as a family. We will give my Older Brother two years to bond with his wife and his son. Now all is well with my brother and his family, as well as with I and my family."

Writing back to his Older Brother, the Younger Brother said, "Older Brother, this is my final letter until we meet again, giving you time with your newfound family. But in two years, we will come together as one family."

After writing this, he gave this letter to a messenger with the words that were necessary to be said, "*troubling past of the Kings*."

In seeing what the message said, all was well. After 18 months of marriage with his Queen, Queen Naveen, he began to dream what was in him were those that had been with him from the beginning, the Different Ones, and it was the head of them who began to speak.

The Murderer said, "Older Brother, why have you and your Younger Brother forsaken your Kingdom to come, turning aside from what is truly yours to be? Because you have allowed yourself and your Younger Brother to rest and decline the Kingdom, I will instruct you on what you must do in order to reclaim the Kingdom. You must tell your Younger Brother that in the state he found his wife, Queen Angana, she must return, proclaiming it throughout the district and the region, taking her clothing and spreading them out in different men's resting places, their abodes, then she and those men are to be publicly hanged. No harm must not come to the Prince Phel'ra; he must be cared for by his father, the Young King, and other women are to take the place of his mother. But for you, Older Brother, the Eldest King, you too must publicly hang your wife, the Queen Naveen, and also her father, your father-in-law. Likewise, like your Younger Brother's son, no harm must not come to your son, the prince, Prince Ker'cill. Now those who came with you must start a rumor, saying that they heard Naveen calling you a King, and you as a King should worship her, and so should this district and her father as a part of this conspiracy. You must act quickly; within seven days, all I have told you and your Younger Brother must be carried out."

The Older Brother cried out, even pleading with the Murderer, saying, "This must not take place, because I and my Young Brother have a family of love."

But all what was said was rejected by the Murderer, because no one else was there for them in their time of tribulations but the Different Ones, as the Murderer was the head of them all. The Older Brother awoke, feeling compelled to comply with what had been said as he awoke from his dream.

The Older Brother began to write to his Younger Brother, and, in detail, told him how he must do away with his wife, Queen Angana. A messenger arrived with a written message from his Older Brother, "*troubling past of the Kings*." He took the message from the messenger happily, then relieved him of his duty. The Young King began to read the message.

As he read the letter, he began to say, "Why has there been no end to the Kings' troubles?" Because he was loyal to his Older Brother, this too must be carried out.

Every day up until the seventh day, they expressed their love for their wives to their wives, also convincing their wives, their Queens, to let their son stay over a few nights with their official's son, and they were to stay there until they went to go and get them. All was agreed by both wives.

Now the seventh day had come and the Young Brother, the King, on the seventh day he began to say in this district publicly, "Love, love I have shown, love has disappointed, and love have betrayed me, the King. Because of this betrayal it must not keep on living, it must die."

So those who came in with the King took hold of the men who had the Queen's clothing placed in their living quarters.

The Queen Angana was placed under arrest to be hanged. While the King continued making his case and charging them, all during the handling of the Queen she began to scream and cry, saying, "Please, I beg for my life and the truth as my eyes see it and my ears hear it, my very soul is in pain and throwing my very mind into severe confusion. How can this be my savior, my love? This is my enemy."

Then she was hanged alongside the men she was accused of, and buried. Now before the days leading up to the seventh day of the Older Brother and the King wife, he had requested that his Queen Naveen and her father go out and reconcile with all the men of power and riches that she didn't take hands in marriage. This would and should keep peace. This would play well into what the King had in mind. Just as the King requested, she and her father did, not knowing that this was part of the King's wicked scheme to be seen by the district in this region and in public, using them as witnesses to make his case. With the rumors that were spreading, concerns rose up by the people so much that the people began to dislike, even hate, the Queen and her father.

So the Older Brother, the King, said, "On behalf of the people, I will act. Bring to me both Naveen and her father."

The men that came in with him, the locals of that district that was filled with anger and hate once they were there in front of Older Brother, the King. He also began to charge them and execute judgment in all what was being said. The father grew angry, demanding the release of him and his daughter, even trying to physically harm the Older Brother. He was restrained.

As for the Queen, she stayed silent and humble, not one word did she speak, only to recall in her mind why he did not want her to expose him as a King to her father. Before the Older Brother came into her life as the perfect savior, this man and his brother had committed such evil acts that she knew exactly who he was.

Just before the King was to carry out the hanging of the Queen and her father, he asked, "Naveen, is there anything you want to say on your behalf to save yourself and only yourself?"

Not one word did she speak to respond to the King, but held fast to her integrity. Then they were hanged and buried.

During the burial of the Queen and his wife, the King had one last act to commit. He began to cry and shout out, "Have I went too far in murdering my wife and my father-in-law?"

Once again, the locals of this district came to his aid, rescuing him from his shouting and tears, saying, "We all have been a witness to your loyalty to your wife and your father-in-law, only for them to deceive you in such a manner. Your charges and judgment are all justified."

Now the Older Brother thanked all the people for their clear thinking, saying, "This has lightened my pain and burden."

After all was said and done, the King stayed around for a few weeks. During his stay, the people did something they had never done before, and that was unexpected.

They came to the Older Brother, saying, "Because of all your pain and suffering, we the people of this district, of this region, have all been moved by you. We have all decided to make you our King. Never have we had a King before, and it is by your laws we will govern ourselves."

By accepting what was being offered, he said, "Then a King I will be. My first act will be to delegate and appoint men of this district, this region, to be preservers of my law and caretakers of it. From this day on, your laws, your traditions, you must continue them, this is my law."

After appointing different men to preserve their ways, he departed himself from the crowd when a messenger of the Young King arrived saying, "*troubling past of the Kings*," handing the Older King a written message

It read, 'All has gone well for me. If this is your position, take this map and meet me there. This is the very place where our Kingdom is to come. This is where it should be built. If you happen to arrive first, please do continue. I have sent the men that craft in iron, metal, gold, silver, wood, and stones there also. I have sent my companion, the record keeper, all ahead of me. So Older Brother, end your stay there, because the time for our Kingdom has come. Leave with the prince and all his caretakers, the woman, and I too will do the same, only my son and highly appointed officer and his caretakers will leave before me and meet you at the place on the map.

Not even giving thoughts on what he should do, the Older Brother, the King, left, but not before saying his goodbyes and saying that he would return. Also, he left with the ones that the Young King had instructed him to leave with.

As they traveled and made it there, he was greeted by all the people that were there, including his nephew. Everyone seemed to be accounted for, except his Young Brother, the King. But just as the Young King had requested, he did start immediately the building of the Kingdom to come. As he laid out the plans to build to all that would be involved in the construction of the building, not only did he announce what a great place to build the Kingdom it was, but he felt a very strong connection to this place.

Now as time had passed, days, weeks, and months, the Older King became concerned about his Young Brother.

The King said to himself, "Has my brother become lost, without anyone to accompany him?"

Distancing himself from the Kingdom to come but far enough to look back at what was taking place, the older King sighed and stared in amazement, taking great pleasure in what he saw in the construction of the Kingdom to come. As he headed back to the construction of the Kingdom, the Older Brother, the King, was met by two men; not messengers but soldiers, saying not the passwords of a messenger, but saying, "Do you know the one who is called Older Brother? Because we have traveled far for our Commander, on behalf of the one they call brother."

At hearing this, he replied and said, "I am the one you are acquiring of. I am Older Brother."

In response, the soldier said, "This has concluded our search. Here, we leave you with a written letter from your Young Brother," and they left.

Now the letter read first, to identifying himself, "*troubling past that of the Kings.*"

'Older Brother, on my way back, I decided to make my journey far less far by traveling through a territory that was military controlled as a common man. There, I was captured by soldiers. On capturing me, I was put in jail and there I remained until my day of sentencing, three days. On the fourth day I was brought in front of, not a judge nor a King, but a commander. A Commander over all the military forces in this territory. In his sentencing, he didn't sentence me to death or prison, but to be his personal slave for many years to come. 20 years. And on that day, I truly will meet with you in our Kingdom, so don't come looking for me, but carry out our wishes.'

After reading the letter, the Older Brother felt much pain and regret, but just as his Young Brother, the King, said, he did honor his sentencing and his courage.

The Older Brother, the King, took 20 years to build the Kingdom to come. In the 20th year, on the day of the young King, the Kingdom was completed. The Older Brother decided that this day should be one of celebration. They did.

While celebrating, the Older Brother said, "Come my son, my nephew, and my brother's closest companion. We will wait in the chamber of the thrones."

While waiting, the companion of the Young King said, "My King, let me make you less anxious on the arrival of your brother, the Young King, by telling you about my travels and all the things made known to me."

In response, the Older King agreed.

"First, my King, I came into this district, a district where I met with these people calling themselves Christian, and they spoke about a different King, one who is eternal with great inspiration. They say, 'Look! The moment of truth has arrived. Death to men's Kingdoms, for the eternal King is among all things new, where destruction has no power, nor death nor sickness.' He has appointed a chief messenger to carry out his words, and to be the leader, an example of all who choose to follow, and even to the ones who don't follow. But all that do follow him to the eternal Kingdom must ask for forgiveness for of all wrong they have committed, be baptized by water, and turn aside from sinful acts, because in his Kingdom only love resides. My King, as I left with all that the Christians had said on my mind, yet I came into another district.

"Now in this district, the locals spoke about many things, but one thing that stayed with the locals was a particular family; a family of three. This family was not from that district, but one from a distant place, keeping to themselves and helping those who were in need. The locals grew to like the family, a mother, a father, and the child, a boy. The father and the boy had a very special relationship. Also, the young boy wore a symbol, a tattoo. This tattoo represented the birthplace of the child.

"While in town one day gathering supplies, the family came in contact with some soldiers. One of the soldiers wanted the mother, to take her as his own, but the mother rebuked the soldier. Doing this brought immediate shame, and resulted in the immediate death of the boy's mother and father. At seeing this, the boy ran, and was only seen from time to time. When seen, the boy was seen talking to himself. They say that because of what the boy saw, the killing of his mother and father before his eyes, this itself brought confusion to the boy's reason, let alone without anyone to love him or to direct him in any such manner of what was right or wrong. Because of this, he was adopted. Adopted by pain. It was pain who divorced the boy from love.

"Now as the boy became of age, he wasn't seen anymore. Some say he left, but other say he died. These two things were held very dear to my heart, but what came next made all things clear, and that was to reason with what was said by the people in those districts, what wasn't known have been made known to me, and what was lost have been found by me through my travels, and what was written by the Kings through their letters. Please, my King, pay close attention to this last but most significant thing about you and your life, because all evidence supports it. What was two is really one, through loss, pain, and confusion. The boy they speak of is you, my King, the Young Brother, and the Older Brother, who later became King, is you.

"Now, because the boy has no other known relatives after the loss of his father and mother, to survive, the boy envisioned another family member to always be with him. A brother. This was who the people had seen the boy talking to, when they say he was talking to himself. A protector that would never leave his side. Perhaps there was one other thing that added to his vision of him having another family member; his name. Brother was the meaning of his name, yes, the meaning of his name. Broderick is his name, which means brother. Yes, this is your name, my King. Broderick.

"Through your written letters to yourself, I have closely examined first the man in your dream, calling himself your closest ally with the concealed mask. He was at the one time your closest ally, and also your father. This lost love only helped you to further yourself in finding what was true. It was you who concealed your father's face in your dream, maybe because of your inner struggles within yourself. When you left the district where your mother and father were murdered to journey throughout the rest of the world, you came in contact with the ways of world, the ones who would parent you in what was bad. You called them the Different Ones, but they were known as the Thief, Liar, Adulteress, and Murderer. They too were abandoned to defend themselves without love or mercy.

"Because there was no change for them in what was good, this became their outlook and practice in life, infecting you and your ways. Now, as for me, my King, it was I that has been your closest companion from the time that I saved your life and you saved mine, to this very day in the wilderness. It was I who took care of you, not a brother, nurturing you back to health. In return, you saved me from my oppressor, the family that enslaved me. In your journey, my King, the thing that was missing in your life came into your life: love. But twice you destroyed it, your wives, Queen Angana and Queen Naveen, because you didn't know how to love or receive love.

"To their death you sent both, because your life had to be based on pain and deception. By now, my King, by me expressing all that as true and evident, you should know that they are not your nephew and son, but both are your sons,

Prince Phel'ra and Prince Ker'cill. This I know, they are your true life of love.

"Now, I will close with one last thing; the Commander that took you is dead. If not, I wouldn't be here talking to you. That has all come to light."

After all that had been said, Broderick the King was speechless, because what was in the dark had come to light not by force, but by truth. The King exiled himself from his Kingdom. Coming to their feet, the brothers, Prince Phel'ra and Prince Ker'cill, spoke, saying, "In all what was said and heard, we, as brothers, shall rule this Kingdom with pure love, with our father's closest companion being our Highest-Ranking Counselor."

THE END

Specially made piece for the King's officers

The Symbol: the tattoo

The Crown

The Crown

The Swords

The Kingdom

CPSIA information can be obtained
at www.ICGtesting.com
Printed in the USA
LVHW041739200120
644175LV00012B/909